WHO'S A PEST?

A Homer Story

WHO'S A PEST?

A Homer Story

By Crosby Bonsall

SCHOLASTIC INC.

New York   Toronto   London   Auckland   Sydney
Mexico City   New Delhi   Hong Kong   Buenos Aires

All rights reserved. Published by Scholastic Inc., 557 Broadway, New York, NY 10012, by arrangement with HarperCollins Publishers. SCHOLASTIC and associated logos are trademarks and/or registered trademarks of Scholastic Inc.

ISBN 0-439-47252-0

12 11 10 9 8 7 6 5 4 3 2 1   3 4 5 6 7 8/0

First Scholastic printing, October 2003

Printed in the U.S.A.

To Plunketts Creek
with love

Lolly, Molly, Polly, and Dolly

all looked at Homer.

Homer was their brother.

"I didn't do it," said Homer.

"Yes, you did," they said.

"Yes, you did. And you're a pest!"

Then Lolly and Molly and Polly

and Dolly all turned their backs.

"Beans," said Homer.

"I'm not a pest."

But Lolly, Molly, Polly,

and Dolly walked away.

Down by the woodpile

Homer said again,

"I'm not a pest!"

"I never said you were,"

said Lizard.

9

"I never said you said I was,"
said Homer.

"I never said you said I said
you were," said Lizard.

"I never said you said I said
you said I was," said Homer.

"Said what?" asked Lizard.

"Said I was a pest," said Homer.

"Who?" asked Lizard.

"You," said Homer.

"Me?" said Lizard.

"I'm no pest."

11

"I never said you were," said Homer.

"I never said you said I was,"

said Lizard.

"Beans," said Homer.

"You started it," said Lizard.

"You are a pest!"

And Lizard slipped away.

"Beans," said Homer.

"I'm not a pest."

He ran all the way

down a hill

and met Chipmunk.

13

"What time is it?"

asked Chipmunk.

"Ten to two," said Homer.

"Ten to who?" asked Chipmunk.

"Not who—what," said Homer.

"Ten to what?" asked Chipmunk.

"Yes," said Homer.

14

"YES," cried Chipmunk.

"What kind of time is that?"

"It isn't the time," Homer said.

"But I asked for the time,"

said Chipmunk.

"I told you," said Homer.

"What?" asked Chipmunk.

15

"The time," said Homer.

"What time?" asked Chipmunk.

"The time it was then," said Homer.

"When was then?" asked Chipmunk.

"Then was when you asked me,"
said Homer.

"When did I ask you?"

asked Chipmunk.

"At ten to two," said Homer.

"But that was then,"

said Chipmunk.

"What time is it now?"

17

"Two to two," said Homer.

"Don't toot at me,"

said Chipmunk.

"You're a pest!"

And Chipmunk ran away.

"Beans," said Homer.

"I'm not a pest!"

18

"No one ever thinks he's a pest,"

said Rabbit.

"You can't tell about yourself."

"I can tell about myself," said Homer.

"*They* can't tell about myself."

"About me," said Rabbit.

"You?" asked Homer.

"They can't tell about *me*,"

said Rabbit.

"You, too?" asked Homer.

"No, you," said Rabbit.

"They can't tell about *you*."

"That's what I said," said Homer.

"Now what shall I do?"

"I'm glad you asked me,"

said Rabbit. "I'm not a pest,

so I shall be able to tell you

how *not* to be a pest."

"Okay," said Homer.

"Stay out of gardens,"

said Rabbit.

"But I don't go into gardens,"

Homer said.

"Well, stay out of them anyway,"

said Rabbit.

"But if I'm not in,

how can I stay out?" Homer asked.

"It's easy," said Rabbit.

"You can stay out by not going in."

"But I *am* out," Homer said.

"You're lucky," said Rabbit.

"You got out in time."

"But I was never in," said Homer.

"Oh, hush," said Rabbit.

"The others were right.

You *are* a pest!"

And Rabbit hopped away.

"Beans," said Homer.

"I'm not a pest!"

Homer sat down.

Soon he heard a sound.

"Help," it said.

"Help! Help! Help!"

Homer looked around.

"Help who?" he asked.

"Help me," said the sound.

"Who's me?" Homer asked.

"Me is me. I don't know
who *you* are," said the sound.

"I'm Homer," said Homer.

"Please help me, Homer,"
said the sound.

"Where are you?" cried Homer.

"Here," said the sound.

"Where's here?" asked Homer.

"Here is here," said the sound.

"Oh, my," cried Homer.

"I'll never find you.

I don't know where here is."

"Then find someone who does,"

cried the sound.

Just then Rabbit came along.

"You must help me," Homer cried.

"Oh, it's you," said Rabbit.

"What a pest!"

"Me is lost," Homer cried.

"You don't look lost to me,"

said Rabbit.

"I'm not lost," Homer said.

"Me is."

"Who is Me?" asked Rabbit.

"You are Rabbit," Homer said.

"I know that," snapped Rabbit.

"Who is the Me you're talking about?"

"He says he is Me," Homer said.

"Well, if he says he is you,"

said Rabbit, "we must find you.

And here you are!"

31

Chipmunk ran by and stopped.

"Please help us," Homer said.

"Oh, it's you," said Chipmunk.

"What a pest!"

"He wants us to find Me,"

said Rabbit.

"Find you?" said Chipmunk.

"You are here!"

"No, no," cried Rabbit.

"Me is here."

"That's what I said,"

cried Chipmunk.

"What did you say?" asked Lizard.

He slipped from behind a tree.

"He said he was here," Homer said.

"Oh, it's you," said Lizard.

"What a pest!

Who's here?" he asked.

"Me," said Rabbit.

"HELP!" said the sound.

"What is that?" cried Rabbit

and Chipmunk

and Lizard.

"That is Me," said Homer.

"You!" they cried.

"No, ME," cried the sound.

"I'm here."

Lolly and Molly and Polly

and Dolly skipped by.

They saw Homer. "Oh, it's you,"

they said. "What a pest!"

But Homer didn't hear.

He and Rabbit and Chipmunk

and Lizard were looking all over.

"What are you looking for?"

asked Lolly, Molly, Polly, and Dolly.

"Not what, who," Homer said.

"Not who, whom," said Rabbit.

"Whom what?" asked the girls.

"Whom are you looking for?"

said Chipmunk.

"We're not looking for anyone,"

said Lolly, Molly, Polly,

and Dolly.

"Well, start looking for ME,"

said the sound.

Lolly took a step back.

Crash!

Lolly wasn't there anymore.

Molly went to look.

Crash!

Molly wasn't there anymore.

Polly ran over.

Crash!

Polly wasn't there anymore.

Dolly ran after Polly.

Crash!

Dolly wasn't there anymore.

"This is silly,"

said Rabbit. He hopped over.

Crash!

Rabbit wasn't there anymore.

Chipmunk went after him.

Crash!

Chipmunk wasn't there anymore.

"Well," said Lizard,

"it's my turn now."

Crash!

Lizard wasn't there anymore.

"HELP!" cried the sound.

"Help! Help! Help! Help!"

cried Lolly, Molly, Polly,

and Dolly.

"Help!" cried Rabbit

and Chipmunk

and Lizard.

"I think I'll go home," said Homer.

But if he went home without

his sisters, his mother would say,

"Well, Homer, where are your sisters?

Where are Lolly and Molly and Polly

and Dolly?"

And Homer would say, "In a hole."

And think of Lizard.

And all the little lizards

waiting for their father.

And their father was in a hole.

And think of Chipmunk.

And all the little chipmunks

waiting for their father.

And their father was in a hole.

And think of Rabbit.

And all the little rabbits

waiting for their father.

And their father was in a hole.

And think of the sound,

whatever it was.

And all the little whatevers

waiting for their father.

And their father was in a hole.

So Homer got them all out.

How? Easy as pie.

This is what he told them:

"Lizard, sit on Chipmunk.

Chipmunk, sit on Rabbit.

Rabbit, sit on Lolly.

Lolly, sit on Molly.

Molly, sit on Polly.

Polly, sit on Dolly.

Dolly, sit on whatever it is

making the sound."

And then—

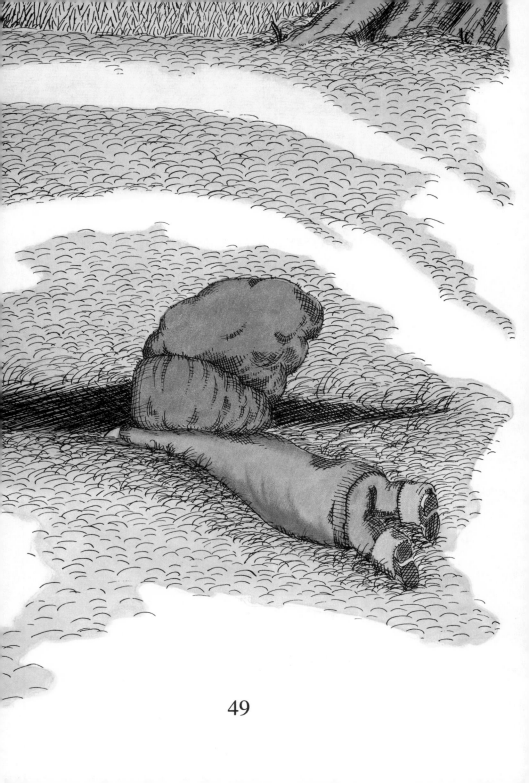

49

Homer pulled Lizard

who pulled Chipmunk

who pulled Rabbit

who pulled Lolly

and Molly

and Polly

and Dolly

who pulled

and pulled

whatever it was.

What was it?

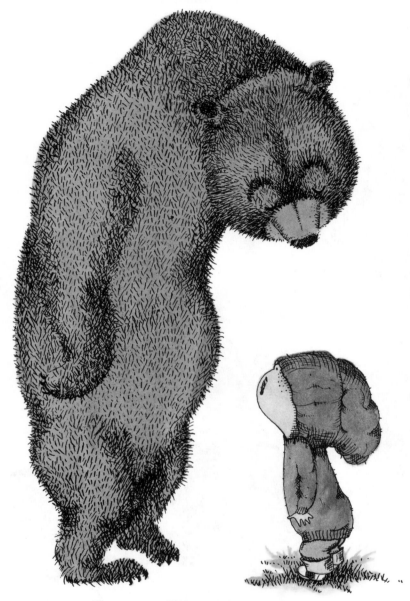

It was Bear.

"I'm a pest," he said.

"No! No! No! No!" said Lolly

and Molly and Polly and Dolly.

"No!" said Lizard

and Chipmunk.

"No, indeed," said Rabbit,

"there's the pest," and he

looked at Homer.

"Not at all," said Bear.

"He got me out."

"He did not. I did,"

snapped Rabbit.

"You did not. I did,"

cried Chipmunk.

"You are both wrong. I did,"

said Lizard.

"No, we did," cried Lolly and Molly

and Polly and Dolly.

55

"I don't see how," said Bear.

"You were all in the hole with me."

"Oh," said Rabbit.

"Mmmm," said Chipmunk.

"Uh," said Lizard.

Lolly looked at the sky.

Molly looked at her toes.

Polly looked at her nails.

And Dolly rubbed her nose.

"Now," said Bear,

"I fell in a hole.

I made a lot of fuss

so—that makes me a pest.

You each fell in the hole.

You each made a lot of fuss.

So—that makes each of you

a pest!"

58

Bear looked at Homer.

"There is just one

who is not a pest."

"Who is that?" asked Homer.

59

"Well, if you don't know,"

snapped Rabbit.

"We won't tell you,"

cried Chipmunk.

"Right," said Lizard.

"What a pest!"

"Beans," said Homer.

"I'm not a pest!"

"Right! Right! Right! Right!"

sang Lolly, Molly, Polly,

and Dolly.

"That's what *I* said," said Lizard.

"Said what?" asked Rabbit.

"Said who?" asked Chipmunk.

"I didn't say anything,"

said Bear.

"We didn't say you did,"

said Lolly and Molly and Polly

and Dolly.

"I didn't say you said I did,"

said Lizard.

"Yes, you did," said Rabbit.

"You keep out of this,"

snapped Chipmunk. "You're a pest!"

Homer and Bear walked away.

"You see how it is," said Bear.

"I see how it is," said Homer.

He looked back.

"Hey," he yelled,

"YOU'RE ALL PESTS!"

Then Homer and Bear

ran off over the hill.

64